For Mike and Elim

First published in the United States of America in September 2015
by Bloomsbury Children's Books
www.bloomsbury.com

Bloomsbury is a registered trademark of Bloomsbury Publishing Plc

For information about permission to reproduce selections from this book, write to
Permissions, Bloomsbury Children's Books, 1385 Broadway, New York, New York 10018
Bloomsbury books may be purchased for business or promotional use. For information on bulk purchases
please contact Macmillan Corporate and Premium Sales Department at specialmarkets@macmillan.com

Library of Congress Cataloging-in-Publication Data
Yoon, Salina, author, illustrator.
Penguin's big adventure / by Salina Yoon.
pages   cm
Summary: Penguin embarks on his next journey—becoming the first penguin to explore the North Pole! Along the
way, he says hello to all his old friends. But when he finally reaches his destination, he realizes he's all alone in a
strange, foreign place. How will Penguin overcome his fears of the unknown and enjoy this new adventure?
ISBN 978-0-8027-3828-8 (hardcover) • ISBN 978-1-61963-730-6 (board book)
ISBN 978-0-8027-3830-1 (e-book) • ISBN 978-0-8027-3831-8 (e-PDF)
[1. Penguins—Fiction. 2. Animals—Fiction. 3. Adventure and adventurers—Fiction. 4. Voyages and travels—Fiction.
5. North Pole—Fiction. 6. Friendship—Fiction.] I. Title.
PZ7.Y817Ph 2015   [E]—dc23   2014047140

Art created digitally using Adobe Photoshop
Typeset in Maiandra
Book design by Nicole Gastonguay

Printed in China by Leo Paper Products, Heshan, Guangdong
1 3 5 7 9 10 8 6 4 2

All papers used by Bloomsbury Publishing, Inc., are natural, recyclable products
made from wood grown in well-managed forests. The manufacturing processes
conform to the environmental regulations of the country of origin.

Penguin's Big Adventure

Penguin was here!

Salina Yoon

BLOOMSBURY

NEW YORK   LONDON   NEW DELHI   SYDNEY

One day, Penguin had a big idea.

He wanted to do something no penguin had ever done.

He wanted to be the first penguin ever to set foot on the North Pole.

Penguin planned and packed.
He rolled up his adventure map
and set off.

But before his first mile,
Penguin saw Emily sewing.

"This looks like a very nice quilt," said Penguin, "and the brightest I've ever seen!"

Before Penguin reached his second mile, he saw his little brother, Pumpkin, weaving.

"That is a fine basket, Pumpkin!" said Penguin, "and the biggest I've ever seen!"

Right before his third mile, he saw
Bootsy braiding the longest rope he'd
ever seen.

Then Penguin set off for the other side of the world, while his busy friends worked on their own world records.

Penguin passed through his favorite places and visited with old friends.

He had a whale of a time!

Finally, Penguin reached the North Pole.

Penguin threw confetti,

turned cartwheels,

and planted a sign.

Penguin was here!

Penguin shouted, "HOORAY!"
and it echoed across the ice.

Nobody answered.

Penguin was suddenly lonely and afraid.

But he was not alone.

Penguin had never
seen a polar bear.

And Polar Bear had never seen a penguin.

It was scary.

Penguin and Polar Bear smiled.
And it wasn't so scary anymore.

Together they went on a North Pole adventure.

built ice forts,

They went whale watching,

explored the Arctic Sea,

and welcomed more visitors!

Then it was time for the
new friends to say good-bye.

Penguin left Polar Bear his adventure map. He didn't need it anymore.

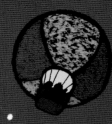

Because the best part of
having an adventure is . . .

. . . coming home!

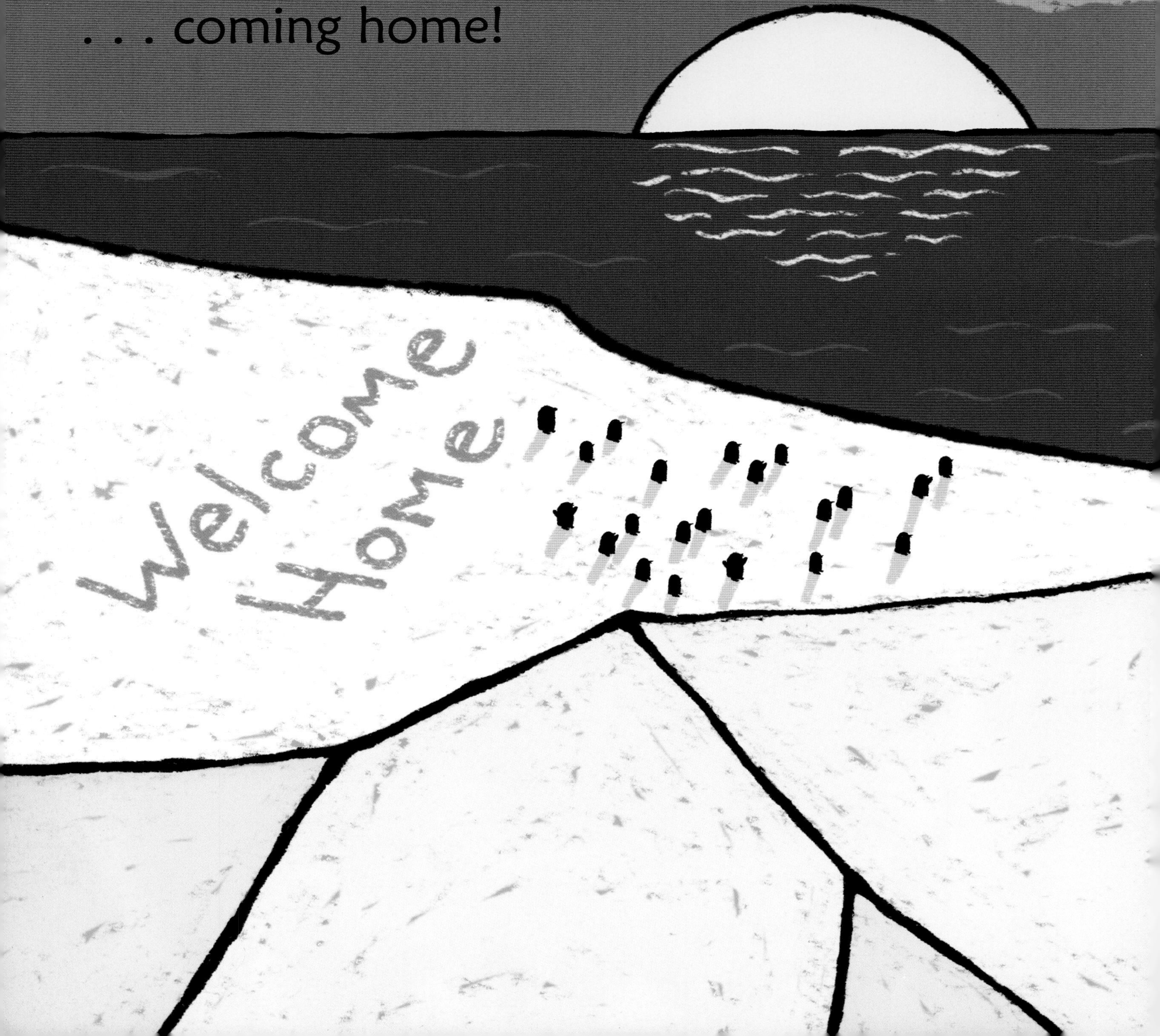

World Record

First penguin to set foot on the North Pole!

Penguin

Certified by Grandpa

Witnessed by Polar Bear

World Record

First polar
bear to meet
a penguin!

Polar Bear
_____

Certified by _____ Grandpa _____

Witnessed by _____ Penguin _____

Arctic Ocean
North America
Pacific Ocean
Atlantic Ocean
South America
N
W
E
S